one

One. Third Edition. (First Edition, 2018).
Independently Published by Melanie Morgan. Guelph, Ontario.

Being one is so much fun!

Each day holds
      something new.

We can't believe how much
you've grown and
all that you can do!

Roll a ball,
spin a wheel,
push a car or truck.

Crawl and
climb and
problem solve
until you are unstuck!

Ring a bell,
bang a drum,
strum a bass guitar.

Dance and clap
and sing along.
You really are a star!

Smile at a friend,
wave bye-bye.
Play some peek-a-boo.

Give a high five,
maybe play shy,
even say a word or two!

Play in the dirt,
squish the mud,
feel garden
and grass so green.

Then wash
and splash
and scrub until
you are so squeaky clean.

Try something new,
explore and chew.
Test out your new teeth.

Then time to wind down,
snuggle in close
for a story and
kiss on the cheek.

So maybe you still take wobbly steps and don't sleep the whole night through...

But being one
is so much fun! And
we're so glad
that you're you!

Author, artist and new mom Melanie Morgan is thrilled for the release of her first children's book. When her son was about to turn one, she searched for the perfect book to celebrate the occasion and could not find one. That is when the idea for One was born. She hopes that other families will enjoy sharing this book together as much as her family does. Melanie lives in Guelph, Ontario with her husband and two children.

Made in the USA
Coppell, TX
06 August 2022

81009493R00021